Prayer to Saint George, the Great Martyr

Holy and Great Martyr,
Saint George the Victorious,
You fought the good fight
and defended the Holy Church
from the wickedness of the evil one.
By holding fast to your faith,
you inspired many
to follow Jesus Christ
as their one true Lord.
Pray for us, St. George,
that we too may have the strength
to fight the dragons in our lives,
and the courage to stand up
for what is right,
what is true,
what is good,
and what is holy.
Amen.

The Saint Who Fought the Dragon

The Story of St. George

Written by Cornelia Mary Bilinsky

Illustrated by Theresa Brandon

Pauline
BOOKS & MEDIA
Boston

Library of Congress Cataloging-in-Publication Data

Bilinsky, Cornelia Mary.
The saint who fought the dragon : the story of St. George / written by Cornelia Mary Bilinsky.
p. cm.
Summary: A fictionalized tale about Saint George, the Roman soldier who defied the emperor's orders to destroy the Christians after imagining himself fighting an evil dragon.
ISBN 0-8198-7161-3 (hardcover)
1. George, Saint, d. 303--Juvenile fiction. [1. George, Saint, d. 303--Fiction.] I. Title.
PZ7.B4928Sai 2011
[E]--dc22
                    2011002905
ISBN:0-8198-7161-3

Illustrated by Theresa Brandon

Design by Mary Joseph Peterson, FSP

"P" and PAULINE are registered trademarks of the Daughters of St. Paul.

Published by Pauline Books & Media, 50 Saint Pauls Avenue, Boston, MA 02130-3491. www.pauline.org

Printed in the U.S.A.

SWFD VSAUSAPEOILL4-110016 7161-3

Pauline Books & Media is the publishing house of the Daughters of St. Paul, an international congregation of women religious serving the Church with the communications media.

2 3 4 5 6 7 8 9   18 17 16 15 14

$\mathcal{I}$t was going to be an unusual day for a brave soldier, but George did not know it yet. He stood in his room, polishing his lance.

"Whatever work the emperor has for me today," he mused, "I'll be ready."

On his way out, George touched the cross that hung around his neck. Quickly, he tucked it under his tunic. It was not safe for a soldier to wear a cross. What would happen if the emperor knew that George was a Christian? "If I keep my cross hidden," thought George, "he'll never know."

Outside, soldiers were gathered around a tall pole, buzzing like bees.

"What's happening?" George asked.

"The emperor has posted an order!" a soldier shouted, "It's about the Christians!"

George turned pale. He thought of the cross he was wearing. Carefully, he read the order. It was worse than he had feared. The emperor was planning to destroy the Christians, and he expected George to help him! Reaching up, he tore down the poster and fled back to his room. George's heart began to pound. He had never disobeyed the emperor's orders. He fell to his knees and pressed his hands over his face.

"Oh, Lord, what should I do?" he prayed.

Many thoughts whirled in his head, and made him dizzy. George felt himself sinking into blackness, down, down, down.

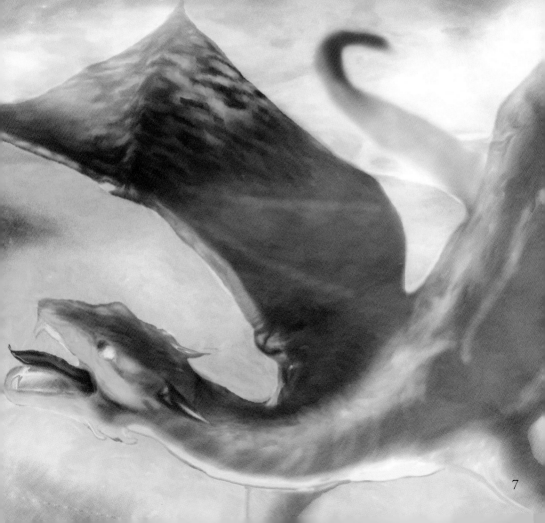

He was in a strange and misty place, riding his horse with his lance at his side. All was silent. Suddenly a loud hissing startled him. A dark green slithery creature was rising slowly out of the mist. It had black horns, red leathery wings, and huge fiery eyes. George shrank back and made the Sign of the Cross.

The dragon spoke.
"You have your orders!"
George gasped as he saw
the dragon's spiked tail. It was
looped around a beautiful lady
wearing a flowing
white gown.

"George!" the lady called, her arms outstretched.
Above her was a golden dome with a cross on top.
In it, George saw terrible scenes. Soldiers were tearing
up holy books. Behind them, a church was burning.
People were fleeing in all directions.

"Help me!" the lady cried. "Be true to the Holy
Church!"

9

"You cannot save the Church!" the dragon roared. "You must DESTROY her!"

"But I am a Christian myself!" George said.

"Nobody has to know! Destroy her!" taunted the dragon.

"No!" cried George, "I cannot do what you want!"

"Then you will lose everything!"

The beast threw its head back and laughed.

11

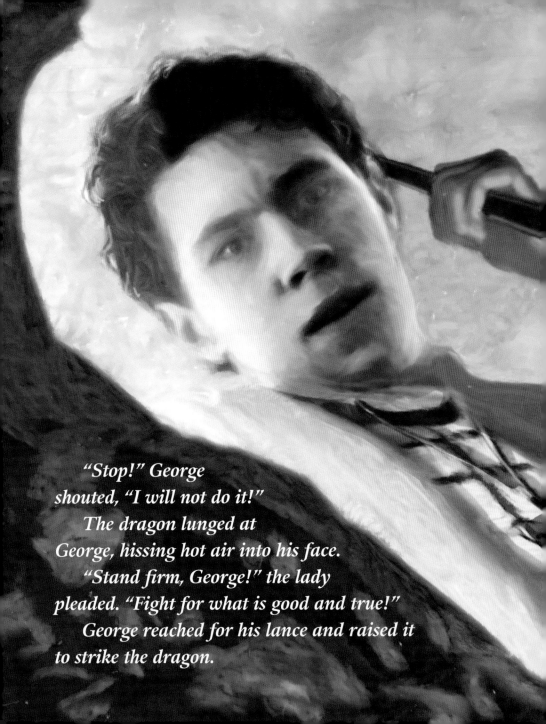

"Stop!" George
shouted, "I will not do it!"
    The dragon lunged at
George, hissing hot air into his face.
    "Stand firm, George!" the lady
pleaded. "Fight for what is good and true!"
    George reached for his lance and raised it
to strike the dragon.

Just then, the dragon's head began to spin. Colors and shapes swirled together and, all of a sudden, George found himself staring into the face of THE EMPEROR!

George dropped his lance. It fell down through the mist and clattered loudly somewhere deep below.

George opened his eyes. He was alone in his room. His lance was on the floor. For a moment, George stared at the lance. Then, calmly, he picked it up.

"Stand firm!" he told himself. "Fight the dragon! Fight for what is good and true!"

George marched to the emperor's palace.

"I want to see the emperor!" he demanded.

The emperor raised his eyebrows when he saw George. "What is bothering my favorite soldier?" he asked.

"This!" George flung down the poster. "Surely you do not mean to harm the Christians?"

The emperor laughed. "What is that to you, George? I don't like Christians. There are too many of them."

George reached under his tunic and pulled out his cross.

"But *I* am a Christian!"

The emperor was stunned, but only for a moment. He shook his head slowly, pretending to be sad.

"George, George! How you disappoint me! You've *always* obeyed my orders!"

"I will not turn my back on my Lord!" George declared.

"Your *Lord*?" the emperor screamed, "But *I* am your Lord!"

"I have only one Lord," said George, "and that is the Lord Jesus Christ."

The emperor's eyes bulged.

"I *am* going to destroy the Christians," he shouted, "and *you* will help me!"

He turned to his guards. "Take him away. You know what to do."

The emperor's guards dragged George to the prison. They took away his lance. They ripped off his tunic. They tore off his cross and tossed it into a corner. They whipped him and left him alone in the dark.

George crawled to the corner of the cell. He found his cross and kissed it. "Jesus," he whispered, "my Lord, my Savior!"

The next morning the emperor sent a messenger to George.

"So you are still alive," the messenger sneered. "You are lucky. Give up this Christian nonsense and the emperor will let you live!"

"No, never," George replied weakly. "I would rather die."

With a cruel laugh, the messenger left.

In the days that followed, George was punished harshly. Still he would not change his mind. After seven days, Empress Alexandria, the emperor's wife, visited him.

"Everyone is talking about you!" the empress said to George. "You have suffered greatly. How can you still stand up to the emperor?"

"I will not turn my back on my Lord and Savior," George answered.

"Lord and Savior?" the empress questioned. "Only the emperor can save you!"

Although he could barely speak, George began to tell her about Jesus Christ, the Son of God who was born on earth, healed the sick, forgave sins, and showed people how much God loves them.

"He died on a cross and was buried, but on the third day he rose from the dead."

George continued, his eyes burning brightly. "And Jesus promised that all who believe in him shall live forever!"

The empress remained silent for a long time. Then she knelt down and touched George's bruised face. Tears filled her eyes.

"Now I understand," she stammered softly. "Your faith gives you this courage. Tell me, how can I become a Christian?"

George looked at her in amazement.

"I know a priest who will gladly baptize you," he said, smiling.

When the emperor heard about the empress's Baptism, he was furious.

"Put that soldier to death immediately!" he ordered, "I will have my way!"

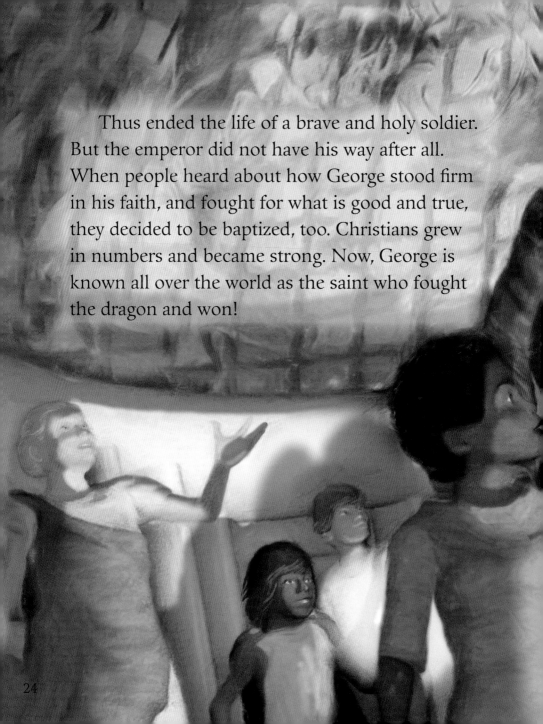

Thus ended the life of a brave and holy soldier. But the emperor did not have his way after all. When people heard about how George stood firm in his faith, and fought for what is good and true, they decided to be baptized, too. Christians grew in numbers and became strong. Now, George is known all over the world as the saint who fought the dragon and won!

*C*ornelia Mary Bilinsky was born and raised in Manitoba. She received her bachelor of arts degree in English and theology from St. Paul's College at the University of Manitoba, and taught English and English as a second language at the high school level. Cornelia's husband is a Ukrainian Catholic priest. They currently reside in Oshawa, Ontario, and have one daughter and one granddaughter. Since 1981, Cornelia has worked alongside her husband at Ukrainian Catholic parishes in Ontario. She most enjoys teaching children about the faith with stories, plays and songs. Cornelia is the author of *Santa's Secret Story* (Pauline Books & Media 2011), and *The Saint Who Fought the Dragon*.

Theresa Brandon has been a freelance illustrator for fifteen years. She has also worked as a children's librarian, an art educator and a theatrical designer. Theresa's interests include reading, family history, antiques, art and theater. *The Saint Who Fought the Dragon* is Theresa's first book with Pauline Kids.

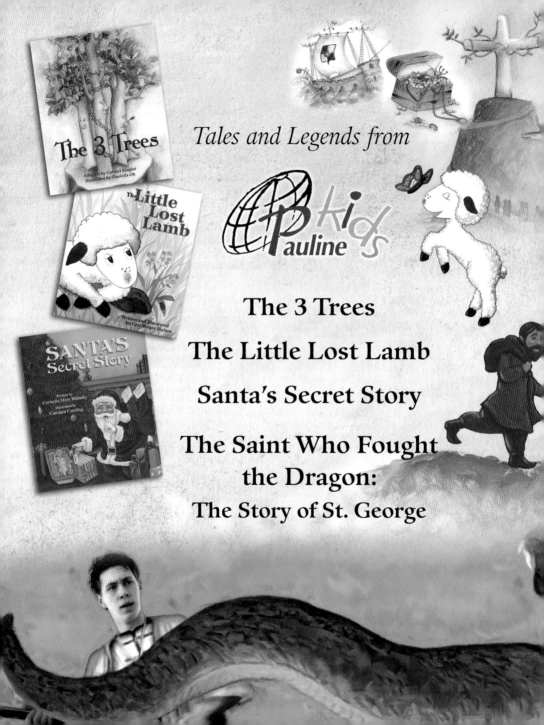

Tales and Legends from

Pauline kids

The 3 Trees

The Little Lost Lamb

Santa's Secret Story

The Saint Who Fought the Dragon:
The Story of St. George

Who are the Daughters of St. Paul?

We are Catholic sisters. Our mission is to be like Saint Paul and tell everyone about Jesus! There are so many ways for people to communicate with each other. We want to use all of them so everyone will know how much God loves us. We do this by printing books (you're holding one!), making radio shows, singing, helping people at our bookstores, using the Internet, and in many other ways.

Visit our Web site at www.pauline.org

auline
BOOKS & MEDIA

The Daughters of St. Paul operate book and media centers at the following addresses. Visit, call, or write the one nearest you today, or find us at www.pauline.org.

CALIFORNIA
3908 Sepulveda Blvd, Culver City, CA 90230 310-397-8676
935 Brewster Avenue, Redwood City, CA 94063 650-369-4230
5945 Balboa Avenue, San Diego, CA 92111 858-565-9181

FLORIDA
145 S.W. 107th Avenue, Miami, FL 33174 305-559-6715

HAWAII
1143 Bishop Street, Honolulu, HI 96813 808-521-2731

ILLINOIS
172 North Michigan Avenue, Chicago, IL 60601 312-346-4228

LOUISIANA
4403 Veterans Memorial Blvd, Metairie, LA 70006 504-887-7631

MASSACHUSETTS
885 Providence Hwy, Dedham, MA 02026 781-326-5385

MISSOURI
9804 Watson Road, St. Louis, MO 63126 314-965-3512

NEW YORK
64 West 38th Street, New York, NY 10018 212-754-1110

SOUTH CAROLINA
243 King Street, Charleston, SC 29401 843-577-0175

VIRGINIA
1025 King Street, Alexandria, VA 22314 703-549-3806

CANADA
3022 Dufferin Street, Toronto, ON M6B 3T5 416-781-9131

St. George

We know that in the first few centuries after Christ, many Christians were persecuted, and martyrs were put to death for their faith. St. George was one of them. It is believed that he was born into a wealthy Christian family in the late third century in Cappadocia (now Turkey). George's parents died when he was still in his teens. After their deaths, he followed in his father's footsteps and became a soldier in the army of the emperor. Because he was so loyal and brave, George was made a commander with the rank of tribune. In the year 302, the Emperor Diocletian ordered the arrest and persecution of Christians. George refused to take part. He presented himself before the emperor, publicly spoke out against this action, and revealed that he himself was a Christian. Though he suffered many tortures, George remained strong in his faith. He was executed in April, 303.

George quickly became a hero for Christians everywhere, and many legends arose giving fantastic accounts of his life. The most famous is the story of St. George slaying a dangerous dragon in order to rescue a princess in distress. Art and icons often show the saint riding a white horse into battle and a dragon representing the powers of evil. In some paintings, St. George's lance is topped with a cross, reminding us that Jesus Christ triumphed over sin and evil. In him, every Christian finds strength.

St. George is the patron saint of many nations of the world. He is often referred to as St. George the Great Martyr or St. George the Victorious. St. George's Cross (a rectangular red cross on a white background), was a popular symbol used by Christian knights during the Crusades and appears on the flag of England.

The feast day of St. George is April 23, the date of his martyrdom.